## Foreword
### Somewhere in Wales – January 2022

Welcome to book 8 of my Outlandish and Poetic wandering through the amazing works of Diana Gabaldon.

It all started almost a year ago, when I dropped a poem onto an Outlander Facebook page and was asked for more. The morning coffee poem has become cherished a fixture on several of the sites. Then I was asked for a book. So, I began publishing – as I went along – and now eight books later here is, Semper in Aeternum (Always Forever).

Along the way I have collaborated with a very talented artist Lynn Fuller – who has allowed me to use her work for cover art and also for page highlights and illustrations. Thank you, Lynn! The result is a series of good-looking books which will grace your bookshelves or side tables,

The contents will remind you of your favourite Outlander bits – Through the whole gamut of emotions and sometimes told with the authors witty, dry, and ribald sense of humour – or so I have been told!

Semper in Aeternum concentrates on the latest book in the series.
Go Tell the Bees that I am Gone.

I have also been asked why RDA (Riding for the Disabled)? – why not a charity connected with Outlander or the cast in sone way
The answer is that Riding for the Disabled is the organisation where I volunteer – I see the work it does with human beings with a multitude of conditions and the positive effects it has on the riders and on the volunteers – it is my passion.
I make no personal income from my writing – all the revenue I generate goes to the two groups where I volunteer – Mount Pleasant, and Bridgend and District. We are small groups but very active and provide a wide range of equine therapies.
Mount Pleasant has also appeared in a short promotional film, promoting Disabled Sport in Wales – this has yet to be released. We are there – in amongst the multitude of activities on offer in Wales.

# Contents

# Earths Workers

Spring – the Bees are waking,
Though they haven't been asleep,
Just buzzing quietly to themselves,
While winter snows were deep,

Gathered in around their Queen
The swarm is of one mind,
Warmer weather coming,
We must see what is to find,

Summer – workers spread their wings,
To their task they strive
Pollinating, gathering,
Keeping the world alive,

The land is bright with colour,
Flowers are in bloom,
Nectar gathered, pollen spread,
For next year's floral boom.

# Semper in Aeternum

## Semper in Aeternum
### Always forever

He loves to quote in Latin,
To exercise his mind,
And now and then a gem is found,
A classic phrase he'll find.

Catullus brings a lifetime back,
Reminders of that moor,
A thousand kisses that have passed,
But never one unsure,

He never feels the pull of time,
For him it is forever
He loved me always in his soul,
Despite my worst endeavour

He accepts mortality,
His faith endures long,
Believes our souls must still survive
Bound as one so strong,

I ask him, how he loves me,
How does he see his part?
For him it was forever,
Right back from the start.

He had no doubts, no second thoughts,
His father to told him true,
He would find the right one,
Or the right one will find you

Semper in aeternum,
For me my Sassenach
Am I now ready in my mind?
To finally quote back,

Semper in aeternum
What words this man can find,
One blood, one bone, one body,
One soul, our life defined.

## Star-bright

We lay out by the fire,
Idly counting stars,
Diamonds spilling 'cross the sky,
Their brightness nothing mars.

Naming constellations,
His knowledge makes me laugh
Warriors and weapons
Even a giraffe?

We reminisce about our lives,
Events that brought us here,
All is tinged by coming war,
With just a hint of fear.

Family returning,
This really is their home,
Exhausted they have gone to bed,
Leaving us alone.

Recall a night so long ago,
His weak and tortured frame,
Cold as ice came to my bed,
Whispering my name,

Desperate in his weakness,
A need to prove a point,
That he could be a man to me,
He creaked at every joint,

Thin, I could feel every bone,
Ghostly like a wraith,
Bright stars seen through a window,
The night that we made faith.

Gone but not forgotten,
She lives inside our hearts,
All is now forgiven,
Since Paris broke two hearts.

# A Gift of Bees

I stopped myself before I hugged,
His beard and clothes alive,
If he were in fancy dress,
He had come as a hive!

John Quincy, always welcome,
No matter how he's dressed
He brings letters for the family,
With bees hung on his chest,

A joyous introduction
Of the family's good friend
An update on his testicles,
All is working at that end!

News from in the city,
For us a source of honey,
And entertainment for the night,
John Quincy Myers is funny.

Bees must have a blessing,
And they must know what goes down,
They must be told of life's events
Or they may just leave town.

Social things, they buzz around,
They keep the land alive,
If we don't look after them,
Then we may not survive.

And so, to feed the waiting hoards,
John Quincy fills his belly,
And will he just decline a dram,
No not on your nelly.

Germain's family miss him,
Home is not the same,
Henri's death was not his fault,
He should not take the blame.

A lengthy social evening,
Letters handed round,
More talk of a militia,
As the whisky haze is found,

And Frances has a letter,
In a formal hand,
A note from William Ransom
From far across the land.

Read out loud in trembling voice,
Afraid to break the spell
Says to thank the Frasers,
Asks if she is well.

The author says he'll write again,
If a messenger do come,
Fannys face lit up and spoke,
Just one word – Will-yum.

## Telling the Bees

The bees are buzzing round the hive,
They don't prevaricate,
A doorway to the spirit world,
Bees communicate.

Talk to the bees and tell them,
Or they will up and leave,
Who is gone, and who is left,
And for who you grieve.

Bees spread word, as they spread life,
They buzz from there to here,
The hive a mystic phone exchange,
To catch a loved one's ear.

Through all time the bees were there,
They hear who tolls the bell,
We tell the bees when hope is gone.
And hope they keep us well.

A phrase evolved since olden times,
An insult and a prayer,
A refuge and a desperate hope,
The bees will still be there.

Who will hold our secrets?
Who can we tell anon,
Will we survive the fall out?
If the bees are gone!

They keep all life together,
With sweet words in the mail,
The hum is but a warning sound
The sting is in the tail.

So, tell the bees when all is lost,
Tell when life moves on,
And when there's no one left to tell,
Tell them that I have gone.

# Earths Workers

Spring – the Bees are waking,
Though they haven't been asleep,
Just buzzing quietly to themselves,
While winter snows were deep,

Gathered in around their Queen
The swarm is of one mind,
Warmer weather coming,
We must see what is to find,

Summer – workers spread their wings,
To their task they strive
Pollinating, gathering,
Keeping the world alive,

The land is bright with colour,
Flowers are in bloom,
Nectar gathered, pollen spread,
For next year's floral boom.

Autumn – leaves are turning
Falling all around,
The trees have thrown their russet cloak,
To cover up the ground,

The hive, alive and buzzing,
Can feel the season change,
The bees can sense the shift of things,
All life will rearrange,

Winter – drives them back inside,
To tell their beehive tales,
Gathered close around the Queen,
Without whom all will fail,

They relive tales of what they heard,
A quiet buzz and hum,
Of what you told them of your life,
The thoughts you shared with them,

Do not think the bees have gone,
When winter comes to stay,
They just doze by their fireside,
And are not out to play.

Be sure and tell them all the news,
Your deepest darkest fears,
For if you don't, they up and leave,
Are gone for many years.

Guardians of all of life,
The world depends on bees,
To keep alive all nature,
The flowers and the trees,

The honey made inside the hive,
Will feed, and soothe, and heal
The taste of all of nature,
Running through each meal,

So, speak kindly to the bees,
When all is said and done,
The balance of the world will fail
When all the Bees are gone.

# Howling at the moon

Unearthly noise, as from a grave,
Loud to wake the dead
A chill ran swiftly down my spine,
My insides felt like lead,

Drawn from bed to window,
To stare into the night,
I knew that noise, it was nae wolf,
Twas nought to give me fright.

Why did it come tae seek me?
Its master had long gone,
Why does it search on this my land?
And sing its mournful song.

Does it call my conscience?
My soul it cannot save,
Or does it guide its master,
Called out from his grave.

Calm yer' selves now children,
It will nae do ye harm,
Alone and lost it seeks a home,
No need for alarm,

I whistled sharp, a known command
She rustled through the trees,
A blue tick hound, pitiful thin,
Howling on the breeze.

A young hound and a rare one,
I knew from where she came,
Twas I that killed her master,
But she did nae carry blame.

Fed and warm and watered,
Bedraggled and dog tired
Petted by the children,
Her tail thumps by the fire.

Tis nae her fault she has no place,
And we will take her in,
Frasers Ridge now has a dog,
A payment for my sin.

A hound will learn with kindness,
In time she will nae roam
Another stray is taken in,
Frasers Ridge its home

# Discretion

I cursed young Ian roundly,
He may have shot the deer,
Ye stay tae do the graloch,
Not just disappear.

Whilst they went off together,
I'm searching on the hill
Where I found a hungry bear,
Feasting on our kill,

It grabbed me by my ankle,
So, I kicked it on the nose,
Then it took my leather shoe,
At least I kept ma hose

It growled a bit and slavered,
I was in retreat,
Bears are lazy in their ways,
Preferring easy meat.

Furry black-haired devil,
With that I will nae trifle,
I will stay here and wait a while,
The fiend has got my rifle!

It's gouged my leg, and ripped ma shirt
And no venison to boot,
Here's hoping Bree and Ian
Had a better turkey shoot!

Ye did'na fight it Uncle,
Bear Killer that's yer name,
I thought ye'd see the bugger off,
Not sit here actin tame,

Young Ian, there's a time and place,
I'm older now and wise,
Bear Killer learned discretion,
And that bear is twice ma size

# Resident Evil

Grapes so sweet and juicy,
Will make a for vintage rare,
We searched for grapes upon the ridge,
Instead, we found a bear,

Vines which drape the hillside
Vines which bear best fruit,
Hanging like a curtain,
Following our route.

Children happy laughing,
Children playing games,
Exploring in the wilderness,
Us calling out their names.

Twas hid behind that curtain,
It's sweet tooth it would slake,
Amy did not see it,
Twas not her mistake.

Jaws of steel clamped on her head,
Its claws ripped through her skin
It growled in rage; its meal disturbed
It tore her limb from limb.

There was no way to save her,
Like Geordie long ago,
I could not staunch the bleeding,
Just ease her letting go.

Find Bobby and the children,
Help them say goodbye,
A wife and mother lost to them,
We watched young Amy die.

Hands clasped in desperation,
Breath rasping through the blood,
The ground was red around her,
Life mixing with the mud.

One eye hardly seeing,
She smiled a smile half blind,
Her last sight friends and family,
As she left her life behind.

Pass the rifle, and call the hounds,
Call the hunters – aye,
A bear has tasted human flesh,
The bear I fear must die.

Cornered up a tree, it fought,
Died at the hands of men,
A creature in whose land we share,
Lies lifeless by its den

Soft warm fur and lethal claws,
Homespun in its teeth
Ferocious, deadly, hungry beast
What beauty lies beneath.

Nothing will be wasted,
Preserved and saved with care.
Food and warmth for winter,
Provided by the bear

## Rebel Soul

Written for my daughter,
For she always will be so,
I helped to raise her, from her birth,
Tis hard to let her go.

The power of curiosity,
Not only killed the cat,
It sends my women back to you,
It does not stop at that.

Yes, I did my research,
I knew you did not die,
I knew she would return to you,
My life became a lie

Read, there is a message
A warning in my text,
Use my research as your guide,
To what will happen next.

I am at your shoulder
As you turn my pages,
Prompting you, the rebel soul,
To read across the ages.

I give our women back to you,
I charge you with their care,
I know that you would die for them,
When I cannot be there.

Rebel Souls the three of you,
You will try to change the world,
Read, you will find guidance,
As your history unfurls

I guided her to bring this book,
There is wisdom in its pages,
Read, I will not lie to you,
From here across the ages.

I do not mean to haunt you,
But you may have me to thank,
Take your place in history,
With Best regards from Frank.

# Broken Sleep

A man I'd known for many years,
But never seen his face,
Stared at me from off the page,
Of the history he chased,

I'd thumbed well through the pages,
He called my rebel soul,
The title likely picked fer me,
He told me of my goal,

Something so familiar
A face which held a cast
At once urbane and civilised,
With shadows from the past

Thief in the night, it broke my sleep
Disturbed my very soul,
One face that hides in darkness
And one whose wife I stole.

Why did she never tell me?
Did she fear a scandal?
That Frank, the man she left for me
Looked like Blackjack Randall.

Faces overlapping,
Watching history play
One a guide to coming war,
One my back would flay

The urge to fight, the urge to flee,
The urge of manhood calls,
Adrenaline she calls it,
That urge that fills ma balls,

I feel for her in darkness,
Desperate for release,
Sorry for just using her,
The act without surcease

I woke at dawn, my mind a blur,
Does James Fraser die?
Frank had written what he found
Claire said he would not lie,

I walked the dawn in solitude,
To clear ma heid of fog,
And thoughts of Blackjack Randall
Just me and Blue the dog.

Ye should ha' told me Sassenach,
The likeness you knew well
One kind, and warm and studious
The other dark as hell.

One above the other,
their faces looked at me,
Would they flog and bugger me to death?
Or invite me in for tea!

Sassenach I'm sorry,
My mind to you was blank,
I'll burn that book, I've read enough,
I've seen enough of Frank.

# Carved with care

It had a certain beauty,
The wood was carved with care
Sanded to a finish
Oiled and polished flair.

Natural and elegant,
The grain swirls round the side,
No rough edges to be found,
Tis finished with some pride,

Reaching in his sporran
The craftsman asks me what?
Is it a toy for Mandy,
Or a teether for a Tot.

Like all his work he's marked it,
Carved with his initial,
Put there for posterity,
Not just superficial.

Who is it for then Sassenach?
I tell him, for old mam,
He looks perplexed and asks me why,
I tell him have a dram,

Old mam has a prolapse,
Its use will be internal,
And old mam might just tell the world,
It was carved by the Colonel!

Two dexterous nimble fingers,
Remove it from my palm
The craftsman exhales gently,
With an air of calm

I think I'd feel self-conscious
He shook his head in doubt,
To have my name upon the thing
Which stops her falling out!

More work it needs then Sassenach,
This carving's not official
The thing that holds her parts in place,
Should not bear my initial

# The Rosary

I rose at dawn tae hunt a bear,
Loaded aye and primed,
Left Claire dozing in the dawn,
With a squeeze of round behind!

No sign of bear up on the hill,
There'd be no fur for coats,
The only one up early here,
Is Jenny and her goats.

I ken she needed salving,
Fer things done in the past,
Long ago forgiven,
But in her mind, set fast.

I told her things she did nae know,
MacCrannoch and Mams pearls,
She told me of her rosary,
To hand down to the girls.

We sat and prayed, for all those gone,
Those we'd see no more
She and I together,
Like in times before.

She with gold, and beads of pearl,
Mine of simple wood,
We sat down and we prayed the beads,
Like all good papists should.

She told me of my ravings,
In the fever of Culloden,
Things I told her happened then,
That I had now forgotten.

We prayed for family and friends,
For loved ones lost and found
We prayed for those in Scotland,
And those dead, on foreign ground,

We prayed for life in time of war
When killing has its say,
That in the hour of our death,
The Lord would ease our way.

She would go with Ian,
On travels to the north,
I would miss her sorely,
She does nae ken her worth.

Wee Mandy she should have the beads,
She'd pass them far ahead,
To the youngest of the line,
If she should end up dead.

Another oath to family,
Another word to keep
She will come back, I know it,
Or I shall never sleep.

Parting with ma sister,
Will take part of my soul,
But the kin folk we remember,
Will strive tae keep her whole.

For services rendered.

When all around is dark despair,
When all your life is sold
Women do what women must,
To try to fight the cold,

We hide our shame,
We sell our lives and do what we are able,
We'd sell our souls to Satan
To put bread upon the table.

Alone with three young children,
She will fight to keep them fed
To raise them up with dignity.
Keep a roof above their heads.

A service done some years ago,
Will not be forgot,
That mustard poultice did its job,
Ifrinn that thing was hot.

That was how Ian found her,
Still living down that road,
A cabin falling round her ears,
And a suspended moral code.

Do whatever..., Jamie said,
See that she is right,
I am forever thankful
For what she did that night.

The customer, a man of note,
Dispatched to meet his maker,
Again, the Scottish Mohawk man,
Is fighting for a Quaker.

The journey north continued,
His band of travellers padded,
His mother and his wife and child,
And four more women added.

Women do what women must,
When it comes to men,
Friend Hardman travels with her girls,
To start her life again.

# The Sachem

He'd come to meet the Honoured Witch,
She who walked through time,
A wise man and a leader,
A man still in his prime,

Is it true he asked me?
Have you conversed with ghosts?
Have you seen them walk the earth?
Do you not fear the hosts?

I told him then of Otter Tooth,
Who travelled with a warning,
A time of war for all the tribes
The end of peace is dawning.

A Sachem, not a healer then,
A chief who led with pride,
Wiseman and advisor,
Until he said – he'd died.

A snake bite sent him to the door,
He'd looked into the light,
His second wife had sent him back,
His time was not yet right.

Since that day he saw them,
Spirits of the past,
Ian Mor at Jenny's side
With two legs, standing fast.

And I had one who followed,
He described Frank to a tee.
He was not there to cause me harm,
He kept a watch on me.

The ghost of he who wrote the book,
Would follow me through hell,
He also stood at Jamie's back,
He followed him as well.

Jamie sensed his presence,
He heard his voice for sure,
In common with the Sachem
He too has seen deaths door

He too had fought his battle,
With venomous attack,
The light had called him to it,
I had called him back

With every death avoided
Each day of life enjoyed
His spirit learns the tongues of ghosts,
Who speak across the void.

# Words of wisdom for William

A career in the army,
An Officer of Rank
Uncle Hal is brief with words,
You have this life to thank!

A man who tells it as it is,
Who does not suffer fools,
But didn't get where he is now
By playing by the rules.

Ruthless in his outlook,
Commanding of respect,
Lord Melton, Duke of Pardloe,
Would have you genuflect.

A well-meant cryptic meaning
A warning about men
The character of colleagues
Outlined with his pen!

Uncle Hal, is always right
He warns you when he must,
Men not to play cards with,
And Captains not to trust.

But will you take his sound advice,
It just might save the day,
Or headstrong with your Fraser blood,
Do it your own way!

# Fireship

Back alleys and brothels,
Enlisted men frequent,
Entertainment far from home,
Their soldiers pay misspent.

To find some female company,
And drink to fill the hours,
Unmindful of the consequence,
These whores don't smell of flowers.

Cleanliness and godliness
Are strangers in this land,
The pox will kill you slowly,
As infection shows its hand.

Fireship is the watchword,
A whore who has the pox
Will have your member burning
Before you leave the docks.

The rash across her body
Plain for all to see,
She plied her trade regardless,
And none of it for free.

Outed by her customer,
The mob will bay for blood,
Demand her death, by fire
Extinguished in the mud.

A fireship set burning,
A cheap life at an end,
Is there no humanity?
Did she have no friend?

He could not stop the burning,
He watched her as she died,
His nostrils filled with scent of flesh,
Which lingered as she fried,

They left her lying on the step
A charred and lifeless heap,
And as the cousins walked away,
They both began to weep.

A sadness for what men became
When faced with acts of war,
And far from home and sanity,
They burned a dockside whore

Such is life around them,
The whores will make a killing,
With scant respect they will infect,
A man whose flesh is willing

## Soul Searching

Searching, always searching
Something or someone,
Always some bit missing,
Incomplete, undone.

Brought up to an Earldom,
Inheriting a title,
I don't feel the joy of it,
That I'm sure is vital.

I am not my father's son,
History will recall
Not Lord John nor the eighth Earl
Share my blood at all,

My father is a traitor,
a Jacobite, a Scot,
Pardoned yes, but criminal
Always a rebel like as not!

Why then would I seek his help,
To free my dearest Jane
To break into a jailhouse,
And see him to feel my pain,

He welcomed in her sister,
No doubts, no questions asked,
His big strong arms surrounded her,
While I my feelings masked.

He says his help is always there,
If my cause is just,
I do not think he offers that,
Lightly, as he must.

Not sorry he's my father,
But sorry for his sin,
He pulls a chord inside me,
But will it draw me in.

Do I want the Earls estates?
How would I make my way?
The lawyers will look after them,
Sort out the day to day.

I've a cousin who's a Mohawk,
But he was born a Scot,
And he has married Rachel,
Fix that – I cannot.

They have a different moral code,
Which runs deep in their soul,
An honesty, a truthfulness,
Should I make that my goal.

Thoughts are whirling in my brain,
I need to sit and think,
Time to set a course in life,
Not teeter on the brink.

I left Frances with the Frasers,
When I rode off that day,
I could so easily have left her,
To live with Lord John Grey.

To see her safe and cared for,
Again, I damn that man,
Will I ever call him father?
That cannot be a plan.

But for now, I'll wait and think,
And search for Cousin Ben,
My bones tell me he is not dead,
Or I'm a Scotsman ken.

## Amaranthus

A name indeed to conjure with,
A pretty little flower,
Elusive and perennial
Short lived in its hour,

A wife, a son, a missing heir,
The Greys are puzzled too.
William will find them,
But is her story true,

Hal protects his family,
From all that lies ahead,
Determined in his stubborn mind
His offspring is not dead.

A shallow grave upon a hill,
A corpse that has no ears,
This is not Ben, this is a thief,
Buried here for years.

Amaranthus swears him dead,
Behaves as though she's single,
Does she know more than she says,
Is she hearing money jingle?

The flirting game she plays with ease
A marriage for a title
Ellesmere's estate is on the line,
It seems that wealth is vital,

She throws her cards at William,
Plays with his emotions,
Would marry him for his estate,
Not for her devotion.

She is adept at playing games,
She knows Ben is alive,
She's playing both sides of the coin,
She knows how to survive.

A meeting purely by chance,
A Quakers wife you seek,
Your cousin wears a coat of blue,
He has turned the other cheek,

Allegiance changed in prison,
The British cause thought weaker,
Ben the rebel general now,
Has changed his name to Bleeker.

The truth of it she always knew
Amaranthus plays the game,
She lies to hide the awful truth,
And save the family name.

Her husband is now lost to her,
Her son an English heir,
Will she keep the facade up?
And does she really care?

## Shades of Red and Grey

A family of Dukes and Earls,
Pillars of the nation
Coats of red and blood of blue,
Through the generations

Loyalty sworn to their King,
British to the core,
Generals and Majors,
Fighting men for sure.

Army life comes natural,
Expected from their birth,
Sons follow their fathers,
All are men if worth.

How will the Duke of Pardloe
Figure what to do?
His son and heir has turned his coat,
Has changed from red to blue.

A crisis then of conscience,
To join the rebel cause
Leave his wife and infant son,
This will get no applause,

Besmirch the family honour
A traitor in the ranks,
Hal will not forgive this,
The family won't give thanks,

But if the war comes to an end,
If the rebels win,
Then Ben could be American,
And cleanse the family sin.

The politics of foreign wars
Fought across an ocean,
Vast expense of gold and men,
Will MPs pass a motion?

Hal is Red, the heir is blue,
And Hal will get his way,
He does not know that plotting,
Will endanger Lord John Grey.

# Gossip and Rumour

Always in the background
Lurking in the dark,
Richardson, the pale grey man,
His features you won't mark.

Unnoticed in a crowd of men,
He is all ears and eyes,
His talent is for intrigue,
He is the king of spies.

Lord John has a secret,
One which could see him swing
Richardson will use him,
Blackmail is his thing.

Gossip to the rumour mill,
Forget the need for truth,
Ezekiel has a stooge in mind,
Percy is his proof.

And why you ask? Where is the need
His target really sure!
Hal must cease his lobbying,
The Crown must win the war.

Ezekiel is a traveller,
He seeks to change a time,
Americans in slavery,
He would end this crime,

The Crown will make it happen,
In all colonial states,
With Coming independence
The Act will come too late.

The Crown must keep on fighting
Despite the vast expense,
Or John may pay a deadly price
For Hal's great influence

# Theory of Time Travel

Ley lines found by ancients,
They marked the places well,
Fissures in the time frame,
Or alleyways to hell,

Learned with superstitious eyes,
Not to venture near
The passages which time has made
The void which they should fear.

In their own times they worshipped,
The seasons and the sun,
Revered the cycles of the moon
And prayed for times to come.

Those places marked with circles,
Stones placed in a ring,
Massive markers form a spot,
Where  old ones dance and sing.

Ancient lore is practiced here,
Sacrifice and blood
Appease the gods, lest all their souls
Be trampled in the mud.

But there are others in their midst,
Those who travel far,
The stones for them a door through time
Sometimes left ajar.

They travel with a purpose,
But cannot change the past,
Their influence already mapped,
From this time to the last.

Time rolls on relentless,
History is writ,
Always by the victors,
And there's the truth of it.

For those who can go back and see,
Both sides of the time
Know that they can't change a thing,
They can't rewrite the crime.

They can but try and tell it,
With fairness and with fact,
And maybe tell the players
To think before they act.

# Reputation

No regrets – how could I have,
For me the war was done,
My men were safe, my wife was not,
Her fight for life not won.

The Monmouth resignation,
Writ in blood and pain,
Deserter, traitor only words,
I feared ye had been slain.

The name of General Fraser,
To Washington would be
A name to have court-martialled
And hung up from a tree.

No longer then a General
The Fraser name is tainted,
They say I up and left ma men
Tae tend my wife – who fainted!

Not one would say it to ma face,
There's some who have that knack,
Tae make the story suit themselves
And stab ye in the back.

Those that know me understand,
The depth of love we share
Not like other women,
There is no one like you Claire.

And I will reap the whirlwind,
Let the Generals talk,
Actions will speak loudest,
They know I will nae baulk.

I din'nae take it lightly
Tae pack my camp for war,
But when I do, I'm ready
To give my life for sure.

The cause is always freedom,
Not to live in chains,
Create a land of fairness,
To salvage what remains.

When they count the bodies,
When death is in the air,
I've faced it all, in times gone by,
They know I will be there

The General who would save his wife,
Did not desert his men,
And Sassenach tae save yer life,
I'd do it all again.

# Once a fox

Tis a stupid fox that does'nae ken
the nature of the foe,
This one was a hunted fox,
Who'd have it on his toe,

A meeting on the level,
There was no level there,
I'll no be staying til the end,
I'm leaving on the square.

I'd left them ay with Arbroath,
Then slipped into the dark,
A wraith into the undergrowth,
Nae leaving a mark.

Pouring rain and thunderstorm
They hunted me through the mud
Sought to end their landlord's life,
I heard the bullets thud.

Nature is a blessing,
All things she'll override,
As I fought them for my life
The earth began to slide.

Cunningham was wounded,
A bullet in his spine,
He'd left me with a cutlass slash,
More sutures will be mine.

Mentally I made a list,
Those men for the Crown,
Cunningham's wee grass snakes,
I bade Claire write it down.

She wrote the names, and cursed them
Devious sons of bitches,
And silently with venom
Continued with my stitches.

Though he can'nae feel his feet,
She'll not leave him to die
Cunningham won't walk again,
Twas not my bullet aye!

She'll tend to all the wounded,
Whichever side they fell,
Our peaceful world is blown apart
All has gone to hell.

Time will heal wounds of the flesh,
I'm feeling that bit better,
I sit and write with saddened hand,
The long eviction letter.

I ken the truth of all of them,
They've surely burnt the bridge,
For Loyalists and their families,
There is no place on The Ridge

Bag and baggage they will leave,
Ten days to quit their spot,
Do not darken Frasers Ridge,
Return and ye'll be shot!

# Laird Have Mercy

Women view things differently
The family view on life,
Home and hearth and children,
The lifestyle of a wife.

Told to leave, in order short,
With children all in tow,
Belongings packed and loaded,
But they have no place to go.

Women always have a plan,
They turn up at the door,
Beg himself for mercy,
Negotiate the score.

My man is not a monster,
Their argument heard out,
He offers them a contract,
A last chance, not to flout.

The rent is with the women,
And all must swear an oath
And if their menfolk break it.
He will evict them both.

Mercy shown and justice,
For those who put their case
The war divided families,
Not all are thrown from grace.

Himself will give them all a chance,
To start their lives afresh,
Loyal now to Frasers Ridge,
Not with the Crown enmeshed.

# Re Birth

Stay - I bid her newborn soul,
Do not leave the room,
Stay – I held her lifeless corpse,
Cradled in the gloom.

Stay – I saw the tears he cried,
Our minds one thought – of Faith,
Stay – there is still something,
This place still holds your wraith,

Warmth – I felt it kindle
Underneath my hands,
Do not leave now little one,
The flame of life commands,

Pulse – I took one heartbeat,
I matched it from my core,
Drew power from my red man
As I had been bid before.

Grow – I fanned the flame of life,
Warmed it with my breast,
Heard the blood rush in my ears
life's rhythm filled her chest.

Hold – we held between us
Balanced on deaths knife,
A Tiny spirit kindled,
And from that formed a life.

Your power will be greatest,
When your hair is white,
He tells me those that frame my face,
Are tinted like moonlight

I could not lose another child,
I forgive my red man's sins,
His strength has helped my inner core,
Save Mrs Cloudtrees twins.

# The Empty Chair

Custom says we save a place
For those who went before,
A seat is saved at table,
Their memory will endure,

.

At Hogmanay ye feel them
The souls who guard our lives,
All those who have gone before,
Husbands, aye and wives,

When my old chair is empty,
Let my spirit not get cold,
Keep me always in your thoughts,
Then let your mind unfold.

I will always be here,
Forever at your side,
As I swore before the priest,
When I made you my bride

When the coming wars are over,
If I do not return,
I will still be here with you,
know I hear you yearn,

Sit with me and share a dram
Wrapped up in my plaid
Bring to mind the night we met,
Don't let yourself be sad

I live forever in your heart,
And when you bare your soul,
I'll hear your thoughts across the void
My spirit keeps ye whole.

What's that ye say? Now Sassenach,
Ye will nae leave my side,
My talisman tae keep me safe,
Ye'll not from battle hide.

Time will come when both of us,
Will need no food to eat,
When that time comes, please tell the weans,
We'll need an extra seat.

Shall we grow old together!
Aye, yer hair is nearly white,
If ye are now a proper witch,
Ye shall nae leave my sight!

Best I find some extra wood,
And set ye on the pyre,
Will ye be needing extra kindling
My feisty heart's desire!!

# Shadows in the Hearth

Shapes in shadows on the wall,
Reflect in tongues of fire,
Lying sated, in the warmth
Of flames and loves desire,

You are a thing of beauty,
I can'nae say too much
Could ye say the same of me,
Do I attract yer touch?

Sassenach I'm gettin' auld,
There's white now in ma hair,
Ma beard is turning scabbit grey,
Do ye still see me fair?

I trace his features in my mind
The scars under my hand,
We've both grown older, such is time,
And time is in command,

I see the streaks of silver,
Where copper once was bright,
But silver shines as brightly,
I'd not care if it was white,

A beauty carved of hardship,
Worn and used by life,
Moulded by adversity,
Tempered by great strife,

My eyes will see you change each day,
My hands and arms will feel,
The force of life within you,
The strength that makes me heal,

Beauty is subjective,
More than in the eye,
And you who fires my very soul,
Your beauty makes my cry.

# Being of sound mind

Parchment spread before me,
My quill poised over ink,
I tapped my fingers on the desk,
It gave me time to think.

I .... I wrote my name is full
Being of sound mind
Then I tried to list the things
My life had left behind.

All my worldly chattels,
Should go – I think it fair,
Apart from some small items,
I leave them all to Claire,

Bequests of land, and mine to make,
If what we know goes down,
Free to leave to whom I choose,
No longer of the Crown.

Bequests of gold for those with sense,
Not tae make a show,
Tae keep it safe and out of sight
From prying eyes who'd know.

What do I leave my one blood son?
He does nae lack for wealth,
I've nothing I can wish him
Except good sense and health.

Deep in thought, my finger taps,
I shall name him as my son,
Acknowledgement made public,
There … the deed is done.

And three casks of good whisky
With which to wash it down,
A hundred pounds in gold to spend,
I write it with a frown.

And he shall have my Bible,
My old green papist book,
Wisdom may he find in it,
If he choose to look.

If I should make heaven,
Unlikely though it seems,
Will I get to see them all
Realise their dreams?

Or will the Lord play games with me
And keep me as a ghost,
That might be fun, I have a list
Of those I'd haunt the most.

I drop the quill and scratch my head,
Time is rolling like a stone
Kings Mountain calls if Frank is right,
I best get this thing done.!

And three requests I have of Claire,
Firstly, find a priest,
To pray for my immortal soul
At the very least.

If wee Davy can'nae travel
If he cannot go back,
Ian must look after him
Keep his life on track.

And I ask ye Sassenach,
Last of all the three,
If this time I don't return,
Please remember me.

# Broadcloth Black

A carrier of messages,
To get a general's ear,
Now standing by The Swamp Fox,
What am I doing here?

Troops aligned for battle,
And me a man of God,
A minister in broadcloth black,
It's all a little odd,

He offers me a rifle,
To take part in this stand,
Give me a sword, but I'm more good,
With Bible in my hand.

How do I comfort fearful souls?
Most of whom will die,
Charging recklessly at guns,
Without good reason why.

Some fight for their freedom,
Some because they're pressed,
Others know not why they fight,
They just followed the rest.

Keep yer calm, and keep yer faith,
Stay behind the line,
No good a dead padre!
So, stay alive is fine!

See the souls of dead men fly,
Hold the hands of those who fought,
Make their deaths not be in vain,
Comfort their last thought.

As death rains down in sheets of lead,
Men trampled on the ground,
Mortar blast and cannon shot,
A killing wall of sound.

Horses scream and writhe with wounds,
Their end will be a shot,
But men will linger on in pain
In mud if not a cot.

Sword in hand and Bible,
The reverend Roger Mac,
A towering source of comfort,
Dressed in broadcloth black.

# Mortality

Will we share some years of peace?
To watch the family grow,
The ridge to thrive and prosper,
The answer – I don't know.

Will we pass our dotage?
Rocking on our stoep,
Watching life through rheumy eyes
Our diet based on soup.

Long nights by the great room hearth,
Listening to the weather,
Long days watching seasons pass,
Growing old together.

I can'nae see that Sassenach,
Yer days are always packed,
With birthings and wi surgery
And yer garden - that's a fact.

And I'm not much fer sittin,
Despite my creaking bones,
As long as ye keep mending me,
I shall not leave ye alone.

I promised when we married,
That I would keep ye fed,
And always with a place tae sleep,
If not always a bed.

As long as I have strength in me,
Tae get up from my seat,
As long as I can fire a gun,
The family shall have meat.

Sassenach we will get old,
We cannot stop the time,
Let's face it now, the two of us,
Are surely past our prime.

Our lives have seen much conflict,
More than our share of war,
Each night I hold you close to me,
I know we will endure.

A life force strong still drives us,
And given better weather,
We'll still ride up the mountain side,
Tae make love in the heather!

To watch ye work keeps me alive,
Yer constant quest for life,
The healing force within ye,
The witch who is ma wife!

What was it Adewayhe said,
When yer hair is white,
Your power then for healing
Will set the world alight.

Hold me Jamie Fraser,
Before we face this day,
I need your arms around me,
As dawn comes out to play.

I think I could do more than that,
I may just make ye smile
With some luck I'll make ye squeak,
And moan in quite some style,

Now quit yer thinking of our age,
For that is but a number,
As long as we have life and breath,
We shall not choose endless slumber.

Always and forever,
In some shape and form,
Bodies joined in Union,
As we see another dawn.

# Kings Mountain

I watched from 'neath a walnut tree,
Its bark peppered with lead
Could not keep track of where he was,
Was he alive, or dead?

Fighting fierce and brutal,
Bayonets at the end,
Men lay bleeding in the grass,
Had he too met his end?

Stop! I grabbed the passing youth,
That rifle is not yours,
Well, he can't use it now, he's dead!
My guts fell several floors.

Body lying in the grass,
Still and cold as stone,
Smeared in blood and leaking life,
Oh, bone of my bone.

Panic, grief, and anger stop!
I have no time to cry,
He's badly hit but breathing, just,
I cannot let him die,

I clung to him, the world went blue,
Hold on, feel my aura
One beat, one breath, keep holding on
Stay with me in the flora,

Iron taste of human blood,
And metal on my tongue,
The musket ball eased from the wound,
Did not reach his lung.

I breathed for him and heard his heart
Synchronise it's beat
Truly now we are one life,
And death we must defeat,

They left us there upon the ground,
The waste of war around us,
As the dawn lit up the sky,
Life finally came and found us.

We were alive, but only just,
The reaper did not call
I watched the chest beneath my hand
It's shallow rise and fall

You are not dead, he raised his head
His eyes blue slits in blood,
The battles done, we're going home,
His whispered answer – good

One in the ribs, one in the knee
One straight through his thigh,
One lodged in his sternum,
Him quite prepared to die,

Ye can'nae die yet papist,
Rogers wise insight!
Ye ken I am a heretic
I din'nae do last rites.

# Snake in the grass

Fierce, fast, ferocious
Frank said it to be fair
Men were falling all around,
Shot whistled through the air,

Reload, fire, reload
I turned to take my aim,
Moved my foot and felt it then,
A gripping stab of pain,

Then I felt each bullet
As it pierced my skin,
And saw the snake wrapped round my leg,
I hate snakes Ifrinn!

Blood and life are leaving,
I'm lying in the brush,
The death that I expected
Coming in a rush,

I can'nae talk, can hardly breath
The darkness starts to stifle
I did not even see the lad
Who came and stole my rifle,

I see the door is open,
My soul heads for the light,
Face down on this battlefield,
Won't see another night

My heart asks for forgiveness
For every living lie,
For every sin committed,
As I prepare tae die.

Ye can'nae save me Sassenach,
I am too weak tae blink
More blood on the outside,
Then inside me I think,

She tends me and she tastes my blood,
What power has she grown,
Blue the light that glows in her,
Her heart beats for my own,

The bullet moves and leaves its hole,
Her blood flows through my veins,
My heart beats slow but constant,
A blue light salves my pains,

I feel her melding to my flesh,
Transferring her life,
Using her own to make mine whole,
This witch that is my wife.

We lie there until morning,
Lying with the brave,
And the rhythmic sound of shovels
As they dig another grave.

Take me home then Sassenach,
I am healing inch by inch
A few more holes, a few more scars
I'll make it at a pinch.

I'll not ask how ye did it,
I suspect ye din'nae ken,
But see yer hair is snowy white,
Look in the mirror hen!

# Surgical fixation

He's sitting on my surgeons' bench,
For surgery on his knee,
To mend a fractured kneecap,
Make his walking free.

If I do not do this,
And do it fairly quick,
You'll spend the time that you have left,
Walking with a stick.

Gold plates from Brianna,
Will hold it all together,
Screwed in place but flexible,
And lighter than a feather.

Screws are of French silver,
Donated now by Jenny,
Taken from her precious watch
That cost a pretty penny.

Tools laid out before me,
The patient troubled deep,
I will nae do it Sassenach,
I might die in ma sleep.

Young Ian - he will hold you down,
With help from Roger Mac,
You will have the anaesthetic,
And I will get you back.

Even if you are strapped down,
You cannot keep it still,
I need that leg immobile
When I go in with the drill.

Can ye guarantee it,
Will ye bring me back.
Give me odds on dying
Convince me Sassenach.

The gambler in him wins the fight,
He submits to the task,
I promise I'll untie him
Before I wake him from the mask.

Stubborn man, determined
To not die in his bed,
Or under anaesthetic
With ether in his head.

# Food for Thought

Land of opportunity,
Where people should be free,
Yet occupied by prisoners
Sent across the sea,

Governed from a mother land,
Whose sole concern is wealth,
Avaricious greedy men,
Rebellion comes by stealth.

A boiling pot of races,
Refugees from wars,
People bound in slavery,
Prisoners and whores.

Tribes of ancient heritage,
With nature hand in hand
Respecters of life's balances
Evicted from their land.

The pot is getting warmer,
About to overboil,
Soldiers sent from cross the sea,
To fight on foreign soil.

The patchwork, threadbare army,
Of those exiled from home,
Will build a land of fairness,
Where all men still can roam.

A land of truth and justice,
Will form in years to come,
Many battles will be fought
Before that day will dawn.

Hard won independence,
But all men must have laws,
Government and bureaucracy
Hold freedoms in their jaws.

But life will run in circles,
And time will outweigh need,
Fair government in all things
Will be replaced by greed.

The fight for freedom still goes on,
By those that pull the yoke,
The heel of greed's oppression
On the neck of simple folk.

The wealthy and the powerful,
Keep the weapons primed,
And poor folk in their millions
Pay for rich folks' crimes.

# There is the Law ......

Tryon wanted men of worth,
Men to keep the peace,
Order in his Backwoods lands
He would have disorder cease.

A bargain that had suited,
A blatant lie to some,
After all there is the law,
And then there's what is done.

And so, a pardoned traitor,
A papist to the end,
Was granted land at Frasers Ridge,
A signature was penned.

In these times of darkness,
When colonies are lost,
Someone will check all the facts,
At someone else's cost.

Ulysses had had heard the talk,
He put it to good use,
With no thought for the Fraser
Who saved him from the noose.

Land obtained dishonestly,
Defrauded from the Crown,
Give up all that you have built,
The gauntlet is thrown down.

Ulysses a landlord,
Would set himself up right,
Taking all the documents,
He rode into the night.

Honest men are hard to find,
Those not swayed by greed,
Though some will spend a lifetime,
Just to pay back one good deed.

A parcel with a stone of white,
Sent to me the healer,
Wrapped in two fine documents,
Stole from the double dealer.


Tryon's deed of what is done,
Original with seal,
And the letter of eviction,
Ulysses – no deal.

# Bearing Witness

Like opposing armies,
Ranged to go to war,
A study full of atmosphere,
We walked in through the door,

The Hardman's and the Higgins,
And all that they inherit,
Battalions of children,
Discuss their parents' merit.

The abandoned, and the widowed,
Have discussed at length,
A merger of their forces,
In numbers there is strength.

Each knows the others history,
Privations they have faced,
Agree to look to better times,
Their families interlaced.

Hardman girls and Higgins boys,
Exchange a relieved look,
The girls at least can boil a stew,
For Bobby cannot cook!

There will be no killing,
'Cept that for the pot,
And no prostitution,
Friend Hardman now need not!

A marriage then decided on,
A union of need,
Friend Sylvia and Bobby
A family indeed.

Past now put behind them,
We witness what they've learned
Sometimes with life you cut a deal,
And forgive the bits that burned.

## To the Hills

One father, captured on a ship,
And anchored out at sea,
An uncle to be blackmailed,
To set his brother free.

The scheming of a Captain.
Politics at play,
I cannot stand aside while fate,
Murders Lord John Grey.

Alone I cannot rescue him,
I need someone to trust,
There's only one man for the job,
Swallow my pride – I must.

Only one man has the skill,
The cunning and the strength,
He and Lord John were good friends,
Could be again at length.

I spurred my horse, and rode for days,
Deep into the land,
Mentally I wrote a speech,
To ask him for his hand.

He swore he'd always be there,
The day that I was born,
He is my blood, I know that now,
But still my heart is torn.

I start to feel more like him,
Than any other man,
Despite my English upbringing,
I am of Frasers Clan.

He's shown me only kindness,
He's there if I should call,
In my mind I know his hands
Will catch me if I fall.

I see the house high on the Ridge,
I organise my words,
I cannot arrive tongue tied,
That would be absurd.

And Frances, yes, I've missed you,
And my sister, and their wife,
I think a lot of Mother Claire,
I too would give my life.

This family of oddments,
Bound by a common strand,
The honour, love, and kindness,
Of a most uncommon man,

I see them all upon the porch,
What welcome will I find,
Already I can feel the force,
The steel inside his mind.

I rein my horse, I have been seen,
My words become a yelp,
In jumbled tones I doff my hat,
Sir, I need your help!

# Christmas on the Ridge

# Explaining Christmas

Ye'd better fetch the bottle,
And if it is nae rainin'
And you can tell me all about
This thing yer mams explainin'

Ye have a tree inside the house,
Ye mean ye keep it whole!
Then ye sit around it
Like some big green totem pole?

Ye dress it up with baubles,
And a star to goes at the top
And shiny stuff called tinsel
And fairy lights, now stop!

Twas Hogmanay in Scotland,
In days when I was wee,
Time to feast and celebrate,
To call on family,

Ye do that too, I'm glad of that
And do ye go tae church,
Even if yer heretic,
Ye celebrate his birth.

Christmas is the birth of Christ,
Who came to save all man,
Papists, oh and heretics,
Included in the plan.

When he was born, he was so wee,
They laid him in a manger,
Kings and shepherds came with gifts,
For a child who lived in danger.

Tell me now of this great man,
Who flies round in a sleigh,
Bringing gifts to girls and boys,
To open Christmas Day,

I dinna want him landing
Up there on my roof,
I've only just nailed down those tiles,
They're slippery under hoof

And climbing down the chimney?
I hope the fires dead,
Can he no land on the floor,
And use the door instead!

I hear yer mother calling,
We'd all best go and see
It's time ye had yer supper,
Just leave some fer me.

I think I'll have another dram,
While I make my plan,
All this climbing on the roof,
Tis not fer this old man,

I think that when ye go tae sleep,
I'm good at creeping round,
Yer granny says I'm like a cat,
I din'nae make a sound.

Yer grand da's good at most things,
He'll give ye a surprise
And if he can't find reindeer,
He may just improvise!

# Christmas Eve

Christmas Eve, we lay in bed,
I drifted into sleep,
Then felt him slide into the night,
Blankets in a heap.

The top drawer of our cabinet,
Is always stocked with food,
Grand da is always hungry,
And always in the mood!

He reached deep into its depths,
For Bannocks, and for cheese,
Then donned his plaid and disappeared,
What was his plan for these?

I looked out of the window,
And saw him in the snow,
Mark the ground with deer hoof tracks,
Just where a sleigh would go.

I asked him where its feet had gone,
That butchered Christmas deer
It had no hooves; they'd been cut off.
He said he'd no idea!

I heard a thump above my head
he climbed up on the roof,
And marked a track across its ridge,
With a stolen hoof.

A glass of whisky by the fire,
A bannock and some beer
A carrot for the reindeer,
A stop for Christmas cheer.

I knew he had been making things,
And there beside his chair,
A single wooden reindeer.
For each child in our care.

And there is one included,
For one we lost, he said,
For Faith is what has brought us here,
Her reindeers' nose is red!

Catlike he returns to bed,
And draws me to his chest,
Cold hands, cold feet to steal my warmth,
His head upon my breast,

Grand da's gifts they'll treasure
More than any toy,
Each one carved with timeless love,
And each one filled with joy!

# Christmas stockings

My ginger cat had done his rounds,
And crawled back into bed,
Cold hands find a warmer place,
His arm under my head,

Muttering in Gaelic,
He says a prayer or three,
Not heard since we went to war,
Far across the sea.

Exploring hands, I sense his need,
Does he never rest,
Lips are soft and soon find mine,
His kisses are the best,

In the dawn of Christmas morn
We lie under our quilt,
The years roll back, inside this womb
The life which time has built.

The house is rousing round us,
The children wake excited,
What has landed in the night?
Their screams of joy ignited.

Grand da, growls and pulls me tight,
A very Scottish noise,
Shall I make him call his Lord,
I know what he enjoys,

The reverie is broken,
By banging on the door
Children's voices burst with glee
They can contain no more!

Sassenach where is my shirt,
The best one without patches,
In the closet, hanging up,
It's with the plaid it matches,

I have no stockings Sassenach,
Where have my good ones gone,
all of them have disappeared,
I've not one tae put on.

He's digging in the clothes chest,
Claire! This is nae funny,
Someone has eaten all of them,
Do socks taste good wi' honey.

Giggling outside our room,
The children being bold,
Hearing Grand Da, hunting socks,
For that they would pay gold.

Sassenach, this is nae fair,
My old ones still are sodden,
I can'nae even find the ones,
I wore last at Culloden.

What was it that ye told the bairns,
Before they went tae bed,
To hang a stocking by the fire,
For that strange old man in red!

Grand da hears ye Mandy,
And Jem outside the door,
Please go and find ma stockings,
Or I'll hang ye up for sure.

A pair of fiends, they bundled in,
And fell upon our bed,
Stockings filled with goodies,
Apples, cheese, and bread

Joyous little faces,
Watch Grand da with glee,
They're hungering for breakfast,
Grand da, is hungering for me!!

# Christmas Morn

Snow lies heavy on The Ridge
It weighs down every bough,
Moonlight glistens in the trees,
All is asleep, for now.

One night of tranquillity,
When all things lie at peace,
All differences are put aside,
In slumbers soft release,

Soon all life will waken,
Christmas Day will dawn,
Life's hive of activity,
Will buzz loud on this morn,

Exited bairns with joyous smiles,
Will rise before their time,
Giggling and merry,
They plot their next great crime,

My arms around the one I love,
I'm warm on this braw night,
My errands done, I draw her close,
I feel the spark ignite.

Laird, leader, landlord
Father, Grand da and Himself
And just for one night of the year,
A red-haired Christmas Elf.

Lying in the darkness,
We truly have one soul,
With her I have no other form,
With her I become whole.

Breaking dawn awakes the ridge,
The crime is truly shocking,
Can ye no help me Sassenach,
Yon bairns have pinched ma stockings!

# Happy New Year

Open all the widows
Open all the doors,
Time to let the old year out,
Time to take a pause,

Raise a glass and make a toast,
This last year is no more,
Drink a dram and see her off,
A strange one to be sure.

Remember though the good times,
There will have been a few,
Every year holds memories,
Move on without ado.

Life is for the living,
Do not be downcast.
Nothing is there to be gained,
From living in the past.

Throw open all your windows,
Open up your doors,
Welcome in a fresh new year,
And start a dream that's yours.

## Other Matters

# Disaster

Last night I dreamed an awful thing
There had been a day,
Bees had not been published,
Season six not on its way,

No new pics of Jamie,
No new pics of Sam,
No Lord John, No white sow
She's finally a ham!

Facebook and the Twitter feed,
Have fallen into silence,
Instagram has broken down,
Are we contemplating violence?

They've cancelled flights to Scotland,
Culloden is no tour,
The Haggis cheers, he can run free.
Across the sacred moor.

An imaginary wasteland
Appeared inside my mind,
I searched inside my cranium,
No words could I find.

With trembling limbs, I crawled downstairs
To try and scratch this itch,
Who had turned Outlander off?
And could I find the switch!

I sudden flash of sanity,
I search my husband's coat,
My disconnected fire stick,
Oh – and here is the remote!

Unsteady hands connect it up,
Searching for the socket,
Is this Jamie's sporran,
Or my husband's left coat pocket.

Power on it springs to life,
And my memory never fails,
He took it to his man cave,
Where Australia lost to Wales.

Life's sweet balance is restored,
I've a Sunday nicely planned,
Outlander on my TV,
And a large dram in my hand

# Hunting Scammers

The Scottish have a standing joke,
About the Haggis season,
Laws laid down for hunting them,
If ye din'nae have a reason,

There should be one for trolling Sam,
There should not be a need,
To infest his life with Scammers
And molest his Twitter feed.

Let's start hunting scammers
Don't believe all you are seeing,
There is no season to hunt Sam,
He is a Heughan being.

# The Celtic Bond

We Celts are most protective,
Of those we love the best,
Our idols and our icons,
We cherish with the rest

We follow them on media,
Defend them to the hilt,
Rally round when stalkers
Try and look under the kilt

Ye can't deny he's handsome,
That sexy blue-eyed smile,
Gazes from those selfies,
He surely has a style,

It's said he's humble, and he's kind,
Generosity complete,
A long string of perfection
Who walks on size 12 feet.

We follow at a distance,
His travels round the world,
Take part in his projects
As each one is unfurled,

His energy is boundless,
A driving force for good,
We'd love to share a dram with Sam
And we know he would.

I think we all get Sam sick
When he flies across the pond,
We like to keep him close to us,
But we have no magic wand.

We hunger for a sighting
A photo if we can.
The lesser spotted Heughan
Is a rare breed of a man.

Let him wander freely,
With a minimum of fuss,
Let him walk the streets in safety,
Then he'll still be one of us.

Don't make fame a gilded cage
High up on some hill,
Allow the man his privacy,
Then we will have him still.

# Joyous Isolation

A time for making merry,
With family all around,
Reflecting on the years gone by,
And those deep in the ground,

The empty chairs at tables,
The ones we loved and lost,
Time to put the world to rights,
And count the human cost.

Think of those without a home,
No roof o'er their heads,
Children sleeping on the street,
While yours are tucked in beds,

Celebrate good fortune,
Enjoy this special day,
In these ever-changing times
it may just fall away,

Appreciate just what you have,
Don't yearn for what is not,
Someone, somewhere would be glad
Of the lifestyle that you've got.

Sitting in your comfy chair,
That last mince pie you cram,
Think of those who sit alone,
As you sip your dram

Think of those with no one,
To brighten up their day,
Take the time to wish them well
It takes no time to say,

This day that now is over,
Was not about the wealth,
In these strange times many folk
Are worse off than yourself,

Make next year a better one,
For everyone you meet,
Humanity costs nothing,
Just get up from your seat!

# Copyright

# Acknowledgements

All this started with the Outlander TV Series which prompted me to join the Facebook page Outlander Books and TV. As a result of the members enjoyment of the first of my poems I continued to write one a day throughout lockdown.  I write them at 6am and they are read at all manner of different times of day around the globe. The coffee time poem has become a fixture.

The source of my material and my inspiration for this series of books has been, the writing of Diana Gabaldon – thank you Diana for being my inspiration without knowing it and for tolerating my use of your work.

Please be assured that every Penny/cent/ brass razoo of what I generate goes to my cause.

The cast and crew of Outlander and the production company – from whose scenes I also draw inspiration.

Lynn Fuller – artist extraordinaire – A master with pastels – who has donated her work to the cause.

As a self-publisher I do not stretch to a team of editors and proof-readers so I would also like to thank

those on the Facebook group who pick up on punctuation and spelling and the odd grammatical howler – and there have been some – always blamed on auto correct! But constructive criticism is always welcome.

Also, to those who actually appreciate my sense of humour which has on occasion been liberally applied to my work.

Thanks, my husband who looks a bit like Dougal but is about as tall as Rupert. A man who now has a complex about tall Scotsmen in kilts.

To our daughter for just being brilliant and threatening to take one of my books to her English Seminars.

To Murph the rescue dog now aged 10 months, who has eaten her share of pencils and dug up 90% of the garden waiting to go for a walk and whose favourite spot is under my desk chair.

And finally, to all the other members of the Facebook groups I joined who have liked my poems and bought them.

# Other Books by the Author

This book is the seventh book in a series of Unofficial Books of Outlander inspired poetry.

Unofficial Droughtlander Relief.

The Droughtlanders Progress.

Totally Obsessed.

Fireside Stories.

Je Suis Prest.

Apres Le Deluge

Dragonflies of Summer

The Blue Vase - In Hardback and Illustrated

I hope the Princess will Approve – a book of COVID and Horse related poems.

Ginger like Biscuits - the adventures of a Welsh Mountain Pony.

Rhymes and Rosettes

Pixie Saves Christmas